Sky jammed a pair of dog ears onto his head and crossed his arms, refusing to get out of the bath

"It's okay to miss your best friend," Mom said. But we have to accept things as they are, even when it hurts."
"But I don't like feeling blue!"
She rubbed his back. "I know it's hard to lose someone you love."

SKY
BLUE

By Adrian Voss

Illustrations by Tincho Schmidt

"How about some ice cream after your bath?" Mom said. "I don't want any ice cream! I want Honeybunny to come back." Sky cried.

When Mom left the bathroom, Sky reached for his shark book. Inside was a photo of his dog Honeybunny.

He imagined they were on a ship sailing away together.

Sky and Honeybunny ran to the front of the ship.
They looked over the railing to see if they could spot
any sharks.
"There's one!" Sky yelled.

They tiptoed below deck in search of food. In the kitchen, Sky and Honeybunny found a pink cake with sprinkles waiting for them.

"Ooh," Sky said. "Let's eat!"

"Want to hear a riddle, Honeybunny?" Sky asked as they munched on the cake. Honeybunny yipped in response.

"What is breezy and pops out of you? Sometimes it tingles in your nose and catches you by surprise. It's really loud, and stuff might come out of your mouth, nose, and eyes...."

A..A...ACHOO!!!

Sky jumped up with a burst of energy, "I wish we could fly to a cookie galaxy with a cape that is a cloud and eat chocolate chip stars and sprinkles that twinkle our way."

"Honeybunny, where are you?"
He searched for her everywhere. Up high, down low,
inside, outside, but she was nowhere.

Sky threw the book onto the floor.

"I can hear you guys whispering!" he shouted.

"I know you're sad, buddy," Dad said.

"I'm not sad. Leave me alone!"

Dad sighed "Sky, nothing really dies, it just changes form."

"So Honeybunny could be a bird now?" Sky asked.

"Maybe," Dad said.

"But will I ever see her again?"

"Honeybunny lives in our hearts and memories forever. Wherever you are, there she is."

After a while, Sky got dressed and walked out to the backyard.
His dad handed him a box.

He peeked in. Honeybunny's ashes were white like sand on a tropical beach.

"Do you want to say anything, Sky?" Mom asked.
He emptied the ashes into the hole. "I love you wherever
you are, Honeybunny."

They stood in silence and listened to the birds chirp goodbye.

"Mom, can we plant a tree for Honeybunny?"

"Sure," Mom said.

"Okay, I think I'm ready for ice cream now."

Made in the USA
Middletown, DE
30 October 2021